WITHDRAWN

Mousie Love

Dori Chaconas   illustrated by Josée Masse

BLOOMSBURY

NEW YORK BERLIN LONDON

Published by Bloomsbury U.S.A. Children's Books
175 Fifth Avenue, New York, New York 10010

Library of Congress Cataloging-in-Publication Data
Chaconas, Dori.
Mousie love / by Dori Chaconas ; illustrated by Josée Masse. — 1st U.S. ed.
p.   cm.
Summary: After falling in love at first sight, Tully the mouse strives to prove his devotion to Frill every
day—while avoiding the cat—but never gives her a chance to respond to his marriage proposal.
ISBN-13: 978-1-59990-111-4 • ISBN-10: 1-59990-111-0 (hardcover)
ISBN-13: 978-1-59990-368-2 • ISBN-10: 1-59990-368-7 (reinforced)
[1. Mice—Fiction. 2. Love—Fiction.] I. Masse, Josée, ill. II. Title.
PZ7.C342Mou 2009   [E]—dc22   2008039888

Art created with acrylic and gel medium on Strathmore Bristol paper
Typeset in Cantoria
Book design by Nicole Gastonguay

First U.S. Edition 2009
Printed in China by Printplus Limited
2 4 6 8 10 9 7 5 3 1 (hardcover)
2 4 6 8 10 9 7 5 3 1 (reinforced)

For Stephanie and Tim, my dearies —D. C.
For Lori —J. M.

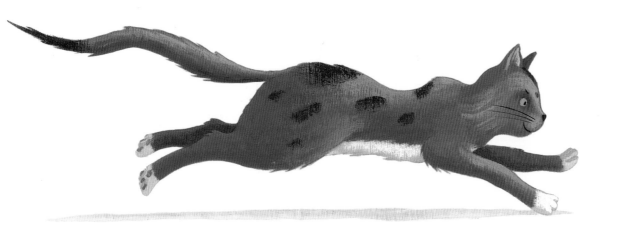

The moment Tully saw Frill, he immediately fell in love.

Tully hadn't planned on falling in love. But the cat had chased him under the pantry door, and there was Frill, in the flour bin, prettily powdered.

With an eager flutter in his heart, Tully didn't say
hello or how do you do? The first words out of
his mouth were, "Will you marry me?"

Frill looked right into his eyes, then smiled.
She held out her paw and said, "Hello. I'm Frill."

"I'm Tully," he answered, taking her floured paw.
Her handshake was warm and snug and, at her
touch, love bloomed more fully in Tully's heart.

"Will you be my bride?" Tully asked.

Frill didn't say no.

She didn't say yes.

She didn't say maybe.

Frill never had a chance to say anything at all.
Because before she could answer, Tully burbled,
"Of course! You must be wondering where we'll
live. I'll find us the perfect house!"

But *where* will I find a house? he worried.

Tully helped Frill squeeze under the pantry door. His heart was in such a flitter, he forgot about the cat. But the cat hadn't forgotten about Tully.

"Run!" Frill yelled.

Tully and Frill skidded and tumbled into an opening under the kitchen stove.

It was pleasant and cozy, and the heat from the oven added warmth. The floor was littered with a delightful assortment of fluff and stuff, just right for nest building. And the cat couldn't reach them.

"Very nice," Frill said, rearranging a few dust balls.
For the rest of the day and night, Tully helped
Frill build a soft, snug nest. And through it all, Tully's
heart melted with love.

When the new-day sun splashed across the kitchen floor, Tully took Frill's hand.

"Now will you marry me?" he asked.

Frill didn't say no.

She didn't say yes.

She didn't say maybe.

Because before Frill had a chance to say anything at all, Tully jabbered, "Wait! You need breakfast! I'll find us some breakfast!"

But *where* am I going to find food? he worried.

Tully saw two large feet in front of the stove—it was the missus, pulling out a pan of blueberry muffins from the oven. Tully saw the cat napping in her basket, and then his eyes settled on two lost blueberries hidden behind a table leg.

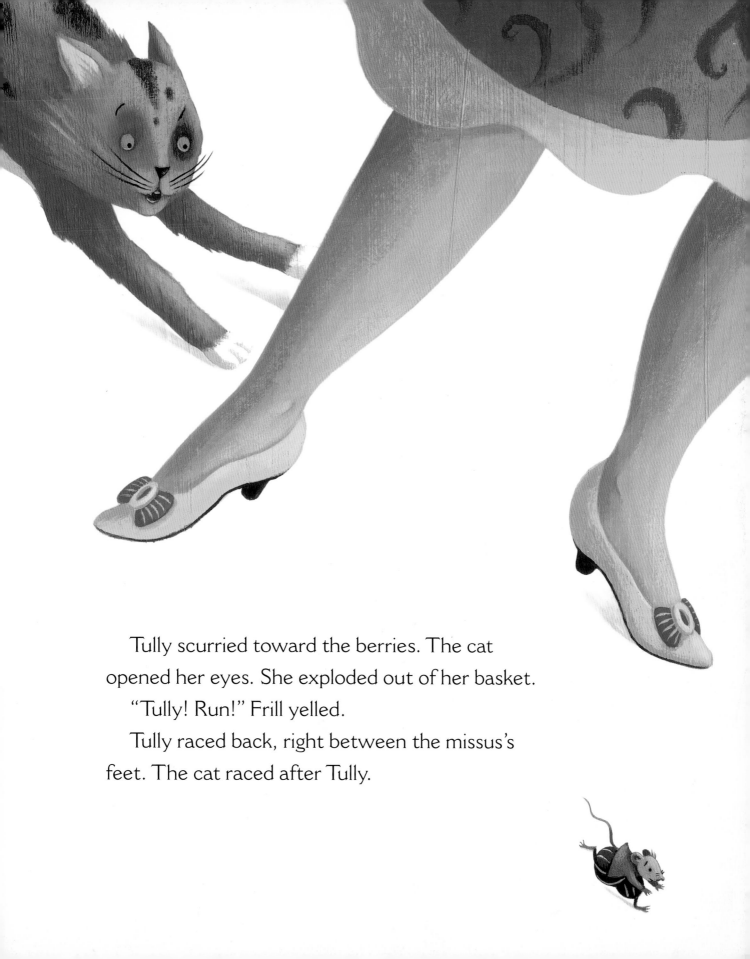

Tully scurried toward the berries. The cat
opened her eyes. She exploded out of her basket.
"Tully! Run!" Frill yelled.
Tully raced back, right between the missus's
feet. The cat raced after Tully.

WHOPPIT! The cat barreled into the missus.
The muffins went flying. One muffin wobbled
to the back of the stove and fell. *THOOOP!*

"A muffin!" Frill said. "Fresh from the oven!"
Tully's heart, pounding from the chase,
pounded even harder with love as they shared
the muffin, nibbling nose to nose.

With every new day, Tully showed Frill his love in a new way. He brought her sugary crumbs, and they talked about their favorite foods. He brought her a blue marble, and they talked about their childhoods. He brought her a daisy, and they talked about their dreams for the future.

"Will you spend the rest of your life with me?" Tully
asked.

Frill didn't say no.

She didn't say yes.

She didn't say maybe.

"Ooooooo!" she said, pointing back toward the kitchen.

The missus was bending down, petting the cat. She
wore a ring with a glittering stone that sparkled and shined.

"A star!" Frill said.

Before Frill had a chance to say anything more, Tully said, "I will find you a shining star!"

But *where* am I going to find a shining star? he worried.

"Tully," Frill said, "I don't need a—"

"We'll wait until dark," Tully interrupted. "We'll find a shining star after the cat is asleep."

The sun went down. The fire in the fireplace
burned out. Moonlight spread across the kitchen
floor, and the cat was asleep in her basket.

Tully and Frill tiptoed around a kitchen stool. The cat was in her basket.

Tully and Frill tiptoed around a potted geranium. The cat was in her basket.

Tully and Frill tiptoed around the wood bin. The cat was *not* in her basket.
"*Meeeoow . . .*"
"Run!" Frill yelled.

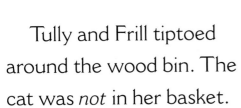

They were near the fireplace.
Tully and Frill scampered into it.
The cat followed.
The mice scurried up the inside of the chimney
to the slanty roof.
The cat followed.

The mice ran to the edge of the roof and stopped
short.

The cat ran to the edge of the roof but didn't stop
at all. Because suddenly she tripped over Frill's foot,
skidded off the roof, and landed in a lilac bush below.

"Ooooooo!" Tully said, looking down at the cat.

"Ooooooo!" Frill said, pointing up at the sky.

The sky was swept with a glitter of stars.
They threw off showers of light like billions
and billions of fireflies.

"So many, many shining stars!" Frill said.
"Thank you, Tully!"

Tully's heart and head overflowed with sweet music.

"Frill," he said. "Will you please marry me?"

Frill put her paw over Tully's mouth before he could say anything more.

"I've been trying to tell you something," she said.

Then Frill didn't say no.

Frill didn't say maybe.

There, under an umbrella of shining stars, Frill said, "Yes, Tully, I will."

And they did.